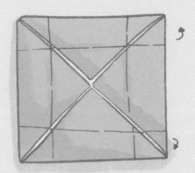

10. Unfold the top and bottom.

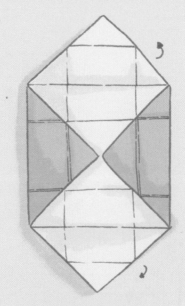

11. Open the top and bottom triangles so the paper looks like this.

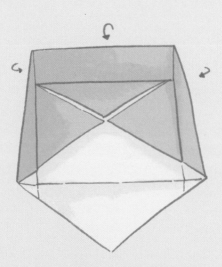

12. Move the top inwards and lift the sides, tucking the folds at the corners inside, to make the walls of the box.

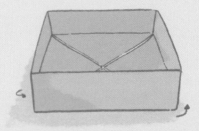

13. Do the same to the bottom part.

14. Now repeat, using a slightly smaller square of paper so that you have a bottom of your box and a lid.

15. Draw your nightmare (make sure it's extra yummy).

16. Put it in your box.

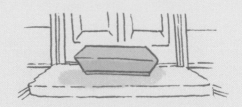

17. Leave your closed box outside your door.

18. If you don't want to make a box, just fold your drawing and address it to the Night Bear.

To Tom and Billie, the tastiest little nightmares

American edition published in 2019 by Andersen Press USA, an imprint of Andersen Press Ltd.

www.andersenpressusa.com

First published in Great Britain in 2019 by Andersen Press Ltd., 20 Vauxhall Bridge Road, London SW1V 2SA.

Text copyright © Ana de Moraes, 2019

Illustrations copyright © Thiago de Moraes, 2019

Distributed in the United States and Canada by Lerner Publishing Group, Inc.

241 First Avenue North, Minneapolis, MN 55401 USA

For reading levels and more information, look up this title at www.lernerbooks.com.

Printed and bound in China by Toppan Leefung Ltd.

Library of Congress Cataloging-in-Publication Data Available

ISBN: 978-1-5415-5509-9

eBook ISBN: 978-1-5415-6058-1

1-TOPPAN-12/1/18

The Night Bear

Ana & Thiago de Moraes

Andersen Press USA

At night, when it's dark and quiet,
the Night Bear hops onto a night
bus and sets off to find his dinner.

Tonight he is in luck.
Lots of children have
left nightmares out.
And nightmares are
the Night Bear's
favorite food.

Monsters with hideous eyes
taste like burgers and fries.

Storms that **bang** and **crash**
taste like sausage and mash.

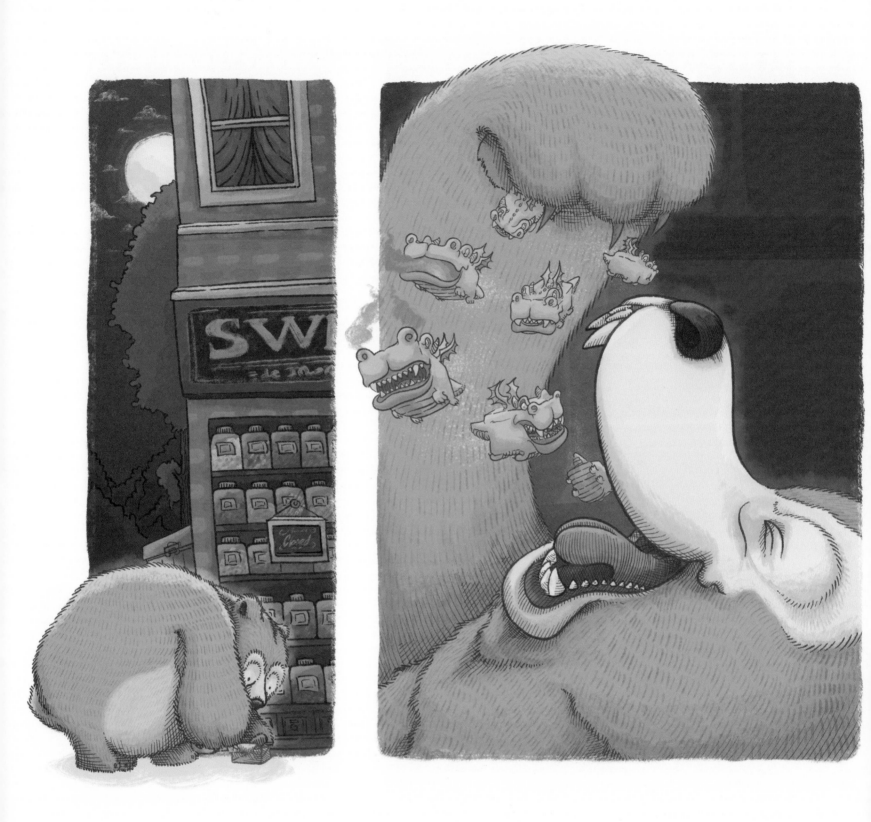

Dragons with a **fiery** bite taste like
Turkish delight.

Scary pirates being **mean** taste like
strawberries and cream.

Unicorns and
rainbows taste
like . . . wait . . .

The night bus will be back soon,
thank goodness. But it does seem a waste
to throw away a whole dream . . .

So the Night Bear goes from street to street,
looking for someone who might like **unicorns and rainbows.**

All the children seem to be asleep.
Until he gets to Tom's house.

He's never seen
a dreamer up
close before.

This one doesn't
have much fur and
is quite small.

He clearly doesn't
eat enough yummy
nightmares.

"Would you like this?"
asks the Night Bear.
"Can I have a look?"
asks Tom.

"Rainbows and **unicorns**!" cries Tom.
"I know," says the Night Bear.
"Really **yucky**."

"Would you like this?" asks Tom.
"It's really horrible."
The Night Bear opens the box...

"Spiders and a giant snake!" (They taste like chocolate cake.)
The perfect pudding to end the evening.

Happy with their new dreams,
boy and Bear say good night.

As the bears wait for the night bus,
the Night Bear tells the others about
his funny new friend, who had fur
only on the top of his head and
a very strange taste in dreams.

And if, like Tom, you are not too keen
on nightmares, then sweet dreams,
sleep tight, hope the Night Bear
comes tonight.

The Night Bear's Favorite Snacks

Cyclopes of doom taste like
delicious mushrooms.

Evil witches taste like
egg sandwiches.

Bats that fly taste
like turkey on rye.

Banshees that scream taste
like custard creams.

A scary yeti tastes like
yummy spaghetti.

Slimy slugs taste like
coffee in mugs.

Scary puppets taste like
chicken nuggets.

Angry gnomes taste like
ice cream cones.

Pterodactlys in the sky
taste like apple pie.

Monsters from the lake
taste like juicy steak.

Giant poodles taste like
ramen noodles.

The Ogre of Fart tastes
like lemon tart.

Bandit queens taste
like baked beans.

Sharks with pointy teeth
taste like roast beef.

Robbers wearing bandanas
taste like ripe bananas.

A howling ghost tastes
like cheese on toast.